Where Is Magenta?

Published by Advance Publishers, L.C.
www.advance-publishers.com

Written by Ronald Kidd
Art layout and composition by Brad McMahon
Produced by Bumpy Slide Books

ISBN: 1-57973-069-8

Blue's Clues Discovery Series

Hi, there! Blue and I are making a scrapbook of her favorite memories with Magenta. Magenta's on vacation, and Blue misses her a lot.

Hey, Blue, where did Magenta go on her vacation?

Oh, I get it! We'll play Blue's Clues to figure out where Magenta went on her vacation! Will you help us? You will? Great!

So what should we put in our scrapbook? Will you help us figure out what we should put in it? Thanks!

Yeah! We can put photographs in the scrapbook. Good idea! Do you see any photos that would be good to put inside?

Oh, yeah! I remember that, Blue! It's a photo of when you and Magenta took a bath. Right! And Slippery blew that really big bubble. That was really cool!

You see a clue? Where? Yeah! The water is our first clue. Good job!

Okay, Blue, what else should we put in the scrapbook? You're going to draw a picture to put in it? Great idea!

Let's see . . . Blue is drawing some trees and lots of colorful leaves. . . .

Oh, I remember that! Magenta came over one day last fall, and we played in the backyard. We raked up the leaves, then ran and jumped in them!

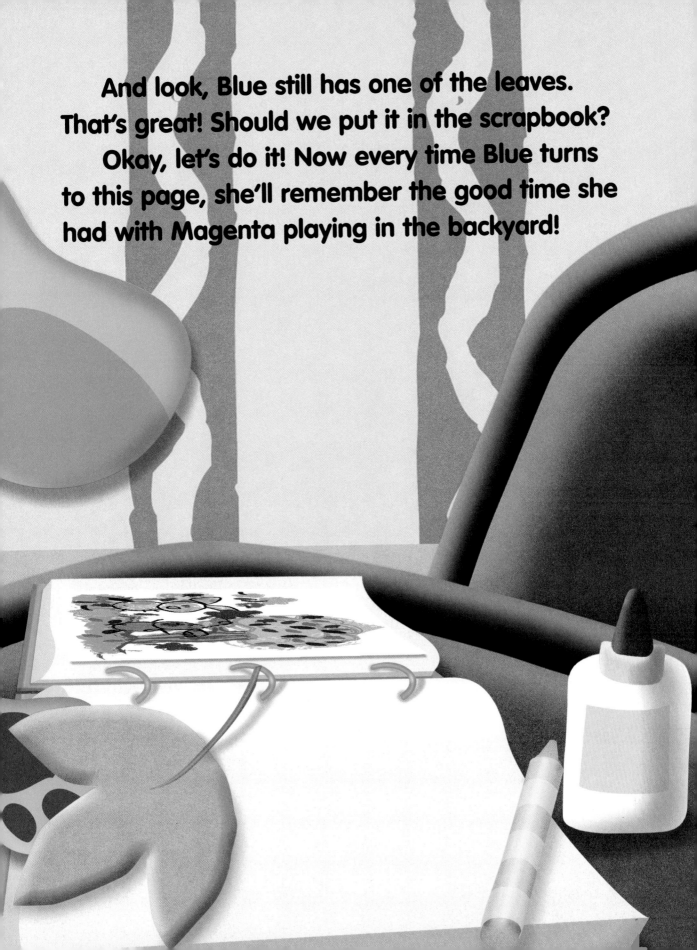

And look, Blue still has one of the leaves.
That's great! Should we put it in the scrapbook?
Okay, let's do it! Now every time Blue turns
to this page, she'll remember the good time she
had with Magenta playing in the backyard!

Oh, wow! Mailbox has a homemade postcard for Blue! Who's it from? Magenta? Great! Let's read what it says. "Dear Blue. Wish you were here. Your friend, Magenta."

I wonder where "here" is. Oh, that's right! We're figuring out where Magenta is by playing Blue's Clues!

What's that? You like Mailbox's sunglasses, too?
Oh! Mailbox's sunglasses are a clue! That's our
second clue! We only need to find one more clue
to figure out where Magenta went on vacation.

What is this sand from, Blue? Oh, yeah! It's from the day that you and Magenta played in the sandbox. Let's tape the plastic bag of sand in the scrapbook!

A pawprint? Where? Wow, you're right! It's on the sand! That must be our third clue! Oh, you know what that means, don't you? Right! It's time to go to our . . . Thinking Chair! Let's go!

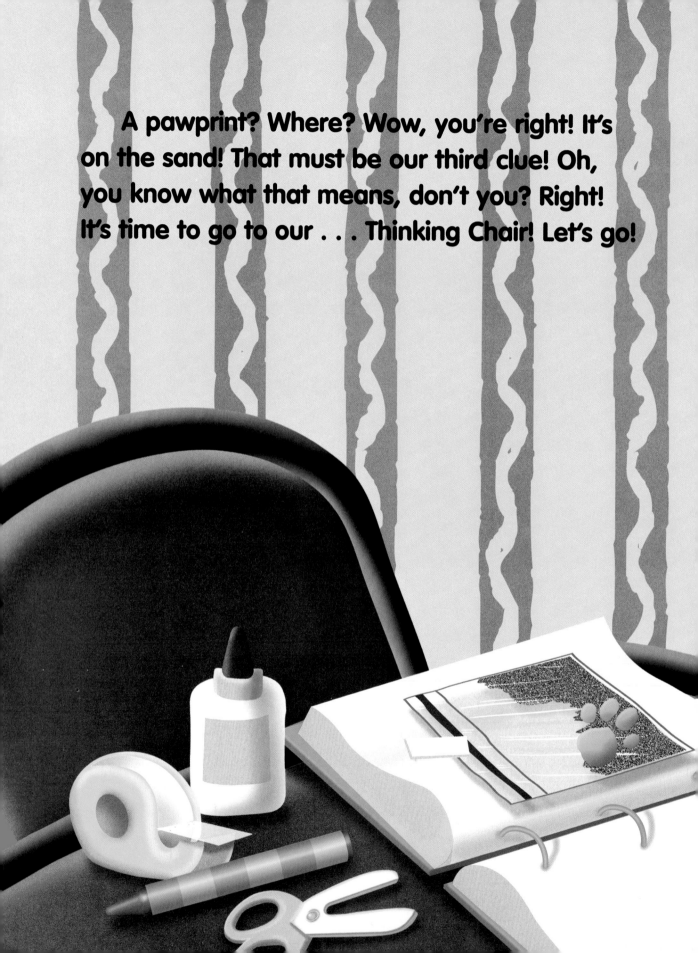

Okay, we need to figure out where Magenta went on her vacation. Let's see. The three clues are water, sunglasses, and sand. So where do you think Magenta could be?

I know! A swimming pool! Oh, you're right—no sand. What about the desert? Oh—no water. Huh? The beach? Water, sunglasses, and sand at the beach? I think you're right!

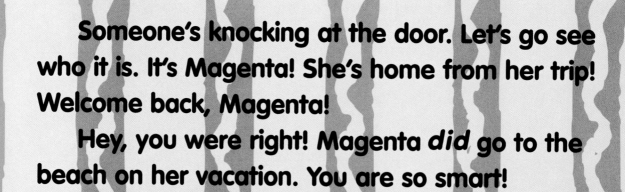

Someone's knocking at the door. Let's go see who it is. It's Magenta! She's home from her trip! Welcome back, Magenta!

Hey, you were right! Magenta *did* go to the beach on her vacation. You are so smart!

Magenta and Blue are having a good time looking at their friendship scrapbook. But the last page is empty.

Oh! Good idea! Blue and Magenta can both draw a picture on the last page. Thanks! What a great ending!

BLUE'S PERFECT POSTCARDS

You will need: scissors, crayons, postage stamps, and a sheet of white poster board

1. Ask a grown-up to cut the poster board into 4" x 5" pieces.

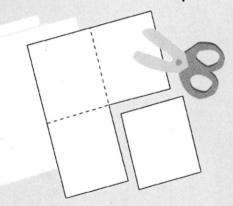

2. Decorate one side of each postcard using crayons, stickers, glitter—whatever you choose.

3. Turn the card over and write an address on the right side and a message on the left side.

4. Put a stamp in the upper-right corner and drop your postcard in the mailbox!